Dear Santa...

All I Want For CHRISTMAS

~~Not~~ A Heartwarming Yuletide Novella

Chuck McKenzie

First published by Daft Notions in 2024
Daft Notions www.daftnotions.com
Melbourne, Victoria, Australia
Copyright © Chuck McKenzie

National Library of Australia Cataloguing-in-Publication data.
All I Want For Christmas
ISBN: 978-0-6458945-4-7 (paperback)
ISBN: 978-0-6458945-5-4 (ebook)

Spelling in this book is standard Australian, which is great value for money as readers get more vowels than they would with U.S. spelling. Think of it as a Christmas gift.

Cover & Interior Artwork by Luke Aldred @lukenotdave
Cover Design & Editing © All In The Edit www.allintheedit.com

Fiction, Science Fiction, Humour

This novella is expanded from a short story of the same title originally published in Confessions of a Pod Person (MirrorDanse Editions, 2005).

With a soft pop of burnt air, Sneet reconstituted in a small, rank-smelling cubicle in a room at the back of the building and found themself sitting in the lap of a rotund, white-bearded, middle-aged human male dressed in a crimson suit almost identical to Sneet's own, clutching a half-full bottle of fluid, with his pants around his ankles. Before the human could cry out, Sneet cocooned him, catching the bottle as it fell. The cocoon writhed on the floor for a moment until the sedatives kicked in. Sneet nodded, then sniffed the open top of the bottle and recoiled.

fermented sugars, their implant whispered. *utilised locally as a beverage, as well as an industrial solvent and fuel*

<Frek! Is it lethal?>

`eventually`

<Why was this information not included in the cerebral download?>

`omissions are inevitable—a note has been uploaded to central`

"Hoy! Stan!"

Sneet looked up. A small, frustrated-looking human male wearing a white shirt with a black tie and slacks stood in the cubicle doorway. The badge pinned to his breast read: HI, MY NAME IS JEREMY. "Just what the heck—?" His expression changed to one of surprise. "Oh, sorry, I thought—I saw you standing there in your Santa suit and just assumed you were Stan, using the loo without closing the door. As usual. Er…do you happen to know where I can find Stan? I was sure I spotted him sneaking in here." He spied the bottle in Sneet's hand. "I certainly hope that's not what I think it is!"

"It is—" Sneet regarded the label on the bottle, "Clan MacGregor Blended Scotch Whiskey, Product of Scotland. But," they added, noting Jeremy's expression, "it does not belong to me."

Jeremy's shoulders slumped. "Well, I suppose I shouldn't be surprised. So where on earth *is* Stan? Any idea?"

"Not here." *Too obvious?* "He went…outside. Of this building." Sneet performed a quick sift through the cultural lexicon downloaded to their cortex. "To have a smoke."

"But…I didn't see him leave the bathroom."

Sneet performed another sift. "He…went out of the window." They pointed towards the small half-open aperture at the top of the wall at the back of the cubicle.

Jeremy's lip curled. "Again? Frankly, it's hard to reconcile his apparent skills in parkour with the fact that he's seldom able to walk in a straight line after lunch." He glanced at the bottle again. "I'm rather surprised we didn't hear an explosion when he lit his cigarette. Unless that's still to come." His eyes narrowed. "What on earth is *that?*"

Sneet followed Jeremy's gaze. *Frek! The cocoon!* Beneath their human disguise, spinnerets tensed, preparing to spray.

"Good Lord!" Jeremy shook his head despairingly. "What *is* this, a gosh-darned *squat?* Cigarettes, alcohol, and now a *beanbag?* Let me tell you, if we weren't so gosh-darned busy, and the agency wasn't so short on Santas this year—" He paused. "You *are* from the agency, I presume?"

Earlier…

Screaming. Flashes of laser-fire. Boiling mud explodes around them. G'norr soldiers fly backwards, reduced to gobbets of seared flesh. The metallic odours of copper and burnt chitin flavour the air. Greasy smoke rolls across the front, lending cover to the fungoid horrors stampeding towards them. Crouching low, Sneet glares down the sights of their maser, squeezing off precise shots as fleeting gaps in the smoke reveal glimpses of teeth and claws and the diabolical glow of atomic weaponry. Enemy combatants burst like microwaved optics, the survivors rapidly closing the gap between the two opposing forces. Sneet switches their maser to a sustained beam and rakes it across the oncoming horde, flaying tissue from cartilage, until the battery drains and dies. Dropping the weapon, Sneet stands and unsheathes the long razorglass blade at their waist as the slathering monsters bear down upon the remaining g'norr troops —

"Well??"

Sneet blinked. "I—apologies, Fleetlord. Could you repeat, please?" The screams of dying soldiers still echoed in their hindbrain.

Kevlaar fixed Sneet with a cold stare. "I *said*…you will accept the mission?" It was barely a question; more a traditional invitation to comply.

Sneet glanced at the light-up display on the conference table in front of them. "Operation Santa?"

Kevlaar waited expectantly.

Refuse! a tiny voice in Sneet's hindbrain whispered. *You are no longer a soldier. You are a farmer. This will take you away from skutcharvest, and if you are not there to oversee the skuttering—*

Unthinkable! interrupted the part of Sneet's mind forged by race and duty and fire. *Refusal is never an option!*

— the smell of burning bodies clogs their olfactory pits —

Frek!

It was being back in this damned place that was causing the flashbacks, Sneet thought; the cold metal underfoot, the overbearing self-importance of military leadership, all awakening the old soldier within. Reactivating the loyal drone. Reviving memories of battle and brutality and bloodshed that

Sneet had long kept repressed simply to be able to function post-service.

Hating themself, Sneet bowed their cranium, taking the opportunity to scan the mission specifications. It was the most basic outline they had ever seen, little more than broad planetary specs and a brief explanation of mission goals. *Why me?* they wondered bitterly. *Dragged from retirement, right in the middle of the most important season of the solar cycle! Surely they have mega-legions of younger, faster, more capable operatives available? They must, at the very least, have plenty of less damaged candidates than I...* "Of course, Fleetlord. I...accept." They hesitated. "But, with the greatest respect, a minor query?"

Kevlaar nodded impatiently, leaning back in their web at the other end of the table. "Anticipated. No, you are not being recommissioned. For the purposes of this mission, you shall remain a 'civilian volunteer'. You will, however, be compensated for your input."

A clawshake from one of the minor Systemlords, in other words, Sneet thought sourly. *And not at all what I was wondering...*

"Now," Kevlaar continued, pointing a claw towards Sneet's display, "you will note this incursion does not follow standard procedure." They paused. "I do not suppose *you* can recall the last time that occurred?"

Sneet made a gesture to indicate they could not, skimming over the specs as they scrolled down their display. A *non-military* incursion? What did that even *mean?* How could subjugation of the indigenous population—reportedly still reliant upon fossil fuels, and indulging in intraspecies warfare—require anything other than an armed invasion when—

Sneet blinked in confusion. "Apologies Fleetlord, but…a Level *Three* civilisation? Surely not?"

Kevlaar nodded slowly. "Confirmed by Central. The indigenes *should* qualify as mere animals. Yet these particular animals have somehow developed atomic and wireless technologies, and even primitive spaceflight, hence the seemingly undeserved classification. Indeed, their technology is broadly compatible with our own, and their existing infrastructure can easily be adapted to our requirements, all of which offers a monumental saving of time, effort and finances—and which, frustratingly, is why we cannot simply obliterate this civilisation from orbit. Furthermore, while we outclass these wretched primates in most respects, our surface-level offensive capabilities are far too closely matched for comfort, which is why a military incursion is out of the question…" They trailed off, glaring at their own display.

There was a short silence, as Sneet considered how to frame their next query in a sufficiently respectful manner. "Begging your pardon, Fleetlord," they said eventually, "but—with the very greatest respect—even taking into account the value of the local infrastructure, why would Central seek to claim this world in the face of such inconvenience?"

Kevlaar pointed again towards Sneet's display. "Subsection five."

Sneet scrolled down to the specified information, then reluctantly nodded their understanding. This world was cited as being ideally and uniquely placed to become the primary forward operations base to facilitate expansion into this entire quadrant of the galaxy, and was thus unarguably vital to the ongoing advancement of the G'norr Dominion. But with such staggering complications preventing the use of standard protocols, how—?

Sneet scrolled further. "Apologies, Fleetlord, but I am not familiar with the incursion protocol cited here."

Kevlaar nodded. "Unsurprising. The 'Deity' protocol has not been employed for many hundreds of cycles. It is an exercise in theatrical nonsense, in my opinion, but has proven successful when required, according to military records. However, to add yet another inconvenience to the list, in this instance we are unable to action the protocol as it currently exists because these primates follow so many distinct and divergent ideologies, with each aggressively opposed to the others, that it completely undermines our ability to infiltrate and conquer by masquerading as a single local deity. This is also why we are unable to impose mass cerebral reprogramming from orbit: the locals are simply too *individualistic*. And setting up full-sized reprogrammers at ground level is out, as local forces would undoubtedly engage long before activation would be possible. Thus, the process must be applied in person, one on one."

One on one??

Sneet opened their mouth to express disbelief. Kevlaar gave them a look. Sneet shut their mouth.

"The extreme value of the planet demands this level of effort," Kevlaar declared. "To this end, operatives will each be equipped with newly-developed, miniaturised cerebral reprogrammers—re-education units—which Central assures us are fully suited to the extreme restrictions of the mission, despite their correspondingly reduced capacity."

Schematics for the REUs flashed up on Sneet's display. *Will these units even be able to tap into the Ego of a species still so developmentally close to being Id-driven animals?* Sneet wondered. *Surely they will simply shake off the effects of the algorithm as easily as any dumb beast would!*

They read on as further information scrolled across the display.

What? WHAT??

'Given the reduced capacity of the REUs, each indigenous subject will require additional personalised reinforcement and embedding of subliminal directives by the supervising operative via cerebral link to their REU, to suit the inferred requirements of the individual subject.'

Frek! Sneet thought incredulously. *But that will take—!*

'Completion of mission estimated at twenty-five local solar cycles.'

FREK!! A full-scale physical military takeover would probably take less than a single cycle!

Kevlaar shot Sneet a look that seemed almost sympathetic. "Be assured, I have expressed to Central my doubts regarding the information you have just noted. But I have been *reminded* that all previously encountered Level Three civilisations were securely bound by the rationality of Ego rather than by the animalistic Id, so even these downsized processors will be able to access the higher cerebral functions of the indigenes."

Sneet nodded unhappily.

"All these obstacles aside," Kevlaar continued, "there is one small ray of starlight peering out from behind the eclipse. The sub-deity for which the operation has been named holds ideological significance for almost forty-five per cent of the indigenous population, and younglings of that percentage are indoctrinated into this ideology also, primarily as a means of behavioural control, which our incursion takes full advantage of."

Sneet nodded again, then hesitated.

"Yes?" Kevlaar asked tersely.

Sneet cringed slightly. "Humblest apologies, Fleetlord. Please know that I intend no disrespect with this query but—honoured though I am to have been considered for this mission—"

"For Freksake! Out with it!"

Sneet took a deep breath. "Well, Fleetlord...I cannot help but wonder...*why?* Specifically, why *me?* That is," they added hastily, "to speak plainly—and I am sure my military records will support me on this—I was never promoted to any rank beyond squadleader, and I cannot imagine that my combat experience lends itself to covert operations of this type. Additionally, I was retired from service a *very* long time ago, so—"

"I agree," Kevlaar interrupted.

There was a long silence.

"I have also looked over the psychological evaluations from your time in service, as well as your ongoing post-discharge assessments."

Another silence.

"There was a time, deep in our past, when veterans with such levels of post-combat neurosis would have been euthanised to minimise risk to society. However, Central, in their infinite wisdom, considers you an essential addition to this operation…despite your involvement being another aspect of the mission about which I have raised concerns. They have, in fact, described you as—" Kevlaar consulted their display again, "—an 'instinctive incursion specialist' owing to your 'highly developed empathic and learning abilities', placing you in the highest percentile of surviving military personnel with regards to your ability to negotiate unfamiliar environments and interspecies communication. Put simply, Central views you as the best of the best, with the numerous commendations, promotions and career opportunities offered to you during and since your service cited as supporting evidence."

Kevlaar paused then leaned forward, their expression darkening. "*I*, however, believe you to be a liability. A uniquely gifted soldier who actively *declined* all honours and advancements? At best, you have clearly never had any inclination towards self-improvement, which disgusts me. At worst you are a coward. Or perhaps even a traitor, unwilling to extend yourself for the benefit of the Dominion."

Sneet kept their cranium bowed, but their mandibles flexed in barely repressed anger. *All I ever wanted was to be a farmer, working the land and livestock alongside my family. But the war machine of Central rolls over everything, chewing up citizens and spitting out soldiers, any notable aptitudes repurposed as weapons. My skills could have been directed into a role in the public sector, or the diplomatic corps, or the medical industry—*

— the clash of blade against blade, claws unsheathed and ready to disembowel —

No! Sneet desperately focussed upon thoughts of their farm, stifling the urge to attack.

"However," Kevlaar continued sharply, "despite *vigorous* objections on my part, Central *insists* that you be among the ten thousand operatives selected for this mission, so my claws are tied."

Sneet made a gesture of respectful acknowledgement. "I am honoured, Fleetlord. And…when is the mission scheduled to begin?"

"Appendix eight."

Sneet scrolled. *Frek!* Immediate *deployment??*

"Yet another inconvenience," Kevlaar grumbled resignedly. "There is an entire season of each local solar cycle devoted to the worship of the aforementioned sub-deity. Regretfully, the current season was well underway before Central noted the strategic importance of the planet, so any delay will result in the mission being pushed back significantly, and this, of course, is completely unacceptable. However, to compensate for the lack of prep time, a cultural lexicon comprising all available intel on this civilisation—behaviours, customs, social miscellany—will be downloaded directly to your frontal cortex. Between that, the support of your implant, and your own noted abilities, Central believes you will be fully equipped to succeed." They fixed Sneet with another cold stare. "So. Be sure to succeed."

The words promised dire consequences for failure.

Sneet bowed again. "As you command, Fleetlord. Earth shall belong to the G'norr Dominion."

The phantom smell of burning bodies tickled their olfactory cilia, then vanished.

"Yes," Sneet said carefully. "I was sent by the agency." In the event that Jeremy decided to check this claim, g'norr A.I.s were standing by to provide confirmation across a variety of indigenous communication platforms.

"Huh. I didn't realise we'd managed to book anyone else, but that's excellent! As far as I'm concerned Stan can go whistle, the worthless—" Jeremy shook his head. "Anyway, mustn't dawdle. Come along, you're on!" He grasped Sneet's sleeve. "And lose the bottle."

Sneet put the bottle down atop the cistern and—after super-magnetising the lock on the cubicle door to ensure Stan's cocoon wouldn't be interfered with—allowed themself to be led from the bathroom and down a series of corridors, finally arriving at a large set of double doors.

"Wait here." Jeremy opened the door a crack and slipped through. A wall of noise blasted through the gap, pummelling Sneet's aural membranes. It sounded like—

— queskin berserkers screeching as they cascade over the top of the trench, sonic cleavers slicing through g'norr troops like c-beams through mist —

Sneet's claws jerked instinctively towards the atomiser tucked into their belt.

`stand down—wait and assess situation`

Focus! Think of the farm!

I miss my farm…

"Well hello, children!" Sneet heard Jeremy call out above the noise. "May I have your attention please?"

There was a susurrus of exaggerated shushing that did exactly nothing to reduce the pandemonium.

"I know you've all been waiting a while, for which Frankston Mall apologises, and we're very grateful for your patience, and I'm very happy to announce that our *very special visitor* from the North Pole has finally arrived! Can everybody tell me who it is?"

"SANTA CLAUS!" screamed the unseen crowd (although Sneet could have sworn they heard a lone voice shout "BLUEY!"). The door flew open. Light blazed in Sneet's optics as they were grabbed by the arm and dragged forth. They blinked, finding themselves standing on the perimeter of a large indoor quadrangle. Before them, a low white picket fence decorated with red-and-white striped poles and clumps of white fibrous-looking material encircled a large, raised dais. A small gate in the fence near to where Sneet stood opened onto a short path which led up to the dais, upon which stood a heavily decorated, high-backed throne. Suspended from the ceiling above the throne was a large painted sign that read 'Santa's Grotto'.

Sneet, who had seen multiple instances of bloody action in grottos, immediately decided that any race too stupid to know what actually constituted a grotto deserved to be conquered.

Beside the throne stood a garishly artificial plant, tall and conical and festooned with long loops of paper that hung from its branches. On the far side of the dais another path led to a second gate, and just beyond that stood a large mob of adult humans, their eyes fixed upon Sneet, a collective expression of (according to the download) aggressive resentment on their faces. And massed about the legs of the adults—

Frek! There are multitudes *of them!*

The crowd of human younglings resembled nothing less than a horde of ravenous grettlers; eyes wide and staring, mouths agape and bawling.

A wave of moist air, heavy with the stench of sweat and hormones and faeces swept across Sneet's cilia—

— drowning in the humidity of the Frelt jungle, firing desperately as their battalion goes down beneath the pincers and leech-tongues of the cthuti swarm —

Sneet quivered, claws inching towards the atomiser.

`delay defensive response—assess situation`

A sharp nudge in the thorax interrupted Sneet's panic attack. "Well? Off you go, then!"

With an effort, Sneet tore their optics from the horde and stared at Jeremy.

"For goodness' sake, give them a wave!" Jeremy hissed.

Relevant information trickled from Sneet's download. Sneet hesitantly raised a claw and undulated their digits. The younglings screeched maniacally.

"What's wrong?" Jeremy demanded. "Why are you being so…*stiff?* Are you *new* at this or something?"

"I am," Sneet admitted.

Jeremy groaned. "Oh for—look, just go and sit on the throne. You can work it all out from there, I hope…"

Sneet slowly walked up to the throne and took a seat, surreptitiously activating the tiny REU unit affixed to their wrist as their implant ran a quick procedural reminder:

younglings sequentially mount santa and re-late their demands—acquiesce to reduce resist-ance to algorithm

<Confirmed. Check output now>

++the g'norr are your friends—welcome them—love, serve, obey—the g'norr are your friends++

output verified

"Nice of you to join us." Sneet started as a small human female suddenly appeared at their side, sneering at them as she pointlessly adjusted a tiny green skirt that barely covered her posterior. "Another liquid lunch?" She blinked. "Oh, sorry! Where's Stan? Who're you?"

"Stan has been relieved of employment. I am John."

"Oh. Well. Okay, John. Keep your hands off my arse and we'll get along just fine." The female bared her teeth at Sneet; a display that anywhere else in the galaxy would have heralded a violent death. Sneet fought the instinctive urge to recoil.

A smile, the download offered. *An expression of welcome and benevolence.*

"I'm Tina, by the way," the female added. "A.K.A. 'Mary Christmas'. Hilarious, huh? Anyway, glad you're here." She nodded towards the crowd, adjusting her skirt again. "This lot's about to riot. So—ready to go?"

"I truly am!" Sneet admitted.

Tina gave them a look.

"…ready to go," Sneet continued unconvincingly, as the download belatedly supplied context, "to the first subject. *Child! Begin.* Ready to *begin* with the first child, I mean."

Tina gave Sneet another longer look. "Riiiiight…"

Sneet cringed inwardly. *Frek! The sooner I get this over and done with, the better. Then I can get back to skutchharvest and—*

Blazing light, as from a low-yield nuclear device going off, seared Sneet's optics.

"ARGH!" Sneet rocked backwards, almost toppling the throne.

— the sickly-sweet stench of melted tallow, bodies burst open by the pressure of the blast —

"Oi! Trevor! A little warning next time?" Tina called out irritably.

Sneet painfully blinked away the flash-blindness and saw a corpulent human male standing a few metres in front of the so-called grotto, fussing over a device that looked suspiciously like an antimatter generator with a large tripod-mounted reflective light projector (*laser cannon?*) standing alongside. Both devices were pointed directly at Sneet, who shrank back into the throne.

*primitive media-recording apparatus design-
ed to produce still images of the target*

Sneet exhaled slowly, claws still tightly gripping the arms of the throne. *<Why was that information not included in the download??>*

*omissions are inevitable—a note has been up-
loaded to central*

The human male glanced up from his equipment. "Yeah, my fault, sorry! I thought Santa already had a kid on his knee!" He waved at Sneet. "Hi, Santa!"

Sneet grudgingly waved back.

"Why aren't you wearing your glasses?" Tina demanded of Trevor.

"Don't need 'em anymore" Trevor called out proudly, clearly addressing the artificial tree to Sneet's right. "Had Lasik surgery!"

"When?"

"This morning!" Trevor beamed.

"Riiiiight…"

"Anyhoo, sorry again. I'll give you a heads-up next time."

"Appreciated!" Tina turned to Sneet. "Ready?"

Sneet shot another look at the waiting mob and nodded tightly. Taking Sneet's response to Tina as a signal, an aging security guard standing nearby shuffled closer. "Why does that guard look so apprehensive?" Sneet asked.

Tina glanced at the guard. "Does he?"

"I can smell his anxiety from here."

Tina shrugged, "Well, I s'pose he's just staying alert. You know, just in case."

"In case of what, exactly?" Sneet demanded, but Tina had already moved away, smiling brightly as she pushed open the entry gate.

"Okay, children!" Tina called, above the din. "Everybody in line? One at a time, please. Who's first?" She reached out, grasped the hand of the nearest youngling, and led him up onto the dais before bending to quietly confer with him. The youngling muttered something. Tina nodded. "Santa, this is Troy."

respond

"Greetings, Troy." Sneet favoured the youngling with a tight smile. The youngling bared his teeth in response. Sneet shuddered.

Silence.

"Troy, aren't you going to say hello to Santa?" Tina asked encouragingly.

"'lo Sanna," the youngling mumbled.

"Come on, up onto Santa's knee!" Assisted by Tina, the youngling scaled Sneet's leg—delivering several optic-watering kicks to Sneet's cloaca—and perched precariously upon their patella. Teeth gritted against the pain, Sneet waited for the youngling to present his demands.

More silence.

prompt required

"So, Troy," Sneet said, "what do you wish me to bring you for Christmas?"

++the g'norr are your friends—welcome them—accept their rule—love, serve, obey++

The youngling chewed his lip thoughtfully, gazing up at Sneet. "Truck?"

A quick sift provided context. "A truck." Sneet nodded. "I believe this could possibly be something I might perhaps supply to you."

linking you to the REU—deliver reinforcement

Sneet glanced at Tina to ensure she wasn't observing them too scrupulously, then leaned in closer to the youngling, staring into his eyes. <*Who do you serve?*> they projected.

The youngling stared mutely at Sneet.

++the g'norr are your friends—welcome them—love, serve, obey++

<*Well?*> Sneet pressed.

The youngling's eyes glazed over for a moment, indicating the algorithm had successfully tapped into whatever passed in humans for a frontal cortex. Then he frowned, hands fidgeting. "The...gnaw?"

<*Excellent*>

embed subliminal directive

<*Now forget all I have said until otherwise directed*>

The youngling nodded.

"Very well," Sneet said loudly. "Go! Await your gifts!"

FLASH!

"ARGH!"

— blinding glare as burning chemicals spray across foliage and soldiers alike, scorching Sneet's optics before their goggles can dim. They scream in agony —

"Sorry!" Trevor called out. "I thought the kid was about to make a run for it!"

Sneet blinked myopically as Tina stepped forward and assisted the youngling in dismounting Sneet's leg. "There you go, Troy. Say goodbye to Santa!"

"Bye, Sanna."

Tina led the youngling to the exit, where two adult humans took possession, smiling and pressing their spawn for information as they walked off towards the photo collection point. Sneet sat back, feeling quite pleased with themself despite their still-smarting optics. They had forgotten the buzz of exercising power over lesser beings; the intoxicating sense of superiority—

— the guttural burp of plasma cannons, enemy troops boiled into fine mist —

Sneet exhaled tightly, refocussing. *This will not be difficult. I shall be back on my farm in no time.*

The next three younglings also proved relatively easy to process (Sneet even remembering to direct their optics downwards to avoid the debilitating flash of the camera), although repeatedly having to reinforce the algorithm quickly became tedious. But Sneet had endured worse in the field, and promises of a toy aeroplane, a 'Barbie' and a 'Nintendo Switch' tripped effortlessly off their tongue while the younglings sat and nodded, eyes glazed as the algorithm sowed the seeds of submission in their minds, before being sent running happily back to their progenitors—

`Parents,` the download offered. `'Father' for male parent, 'Mother' for female.`

And then—

"You're not the *real* Santa!"

Sneet jerked in panic, almost tipping the sneering youngling off their leg as they grabbed for their atomiser. *Discovered!*

delay defensive response—await confirmation of hostile intent

"Of *course* he's the real Santa, Charles." Tina laid a supportive hand on Sneet's shoulder. "Isn't that right, Santa?"

Sneet nodded, pulmonary glands pulsing furiously. "Yes. I am the real Santa." They forced a smile. "Why would you think otherwise?"

The youngling probed his nasal orifice with a practised finger. "My brother says you're not the real Santa, 'cos if you're the real Santa then how come they got a Santa over at Southlands who says *he's* the real Santa, and the Langwarrin mall too, and you can't *all* be the real Santa, so he says you're all lying and *none* of you is the real Santa." Charles paused, examining a lump of something unthinkable wedged under his fingernail. "You're a *faker!*"

Against all logic, Sneet felt personally affronted by the accusation. "I am not a faker," they said, stiffly. "I am the genuine Santa."

"Are not."

"I am."

"Not!"

"Am!"

"NOT!"

"AM!!!"

Charles favoured Sneet with an expression of contempt worthy of a g'norr drill instructor. *"Prove* it!"

Sneet considered. "Very well. Tell me, how is it that I am able to visit all homes upon this world on a single night of the year?"

A careless shrug. "Magic."

"That…is correct. So, if I employ *magic*," Sneet continued, unable to keep the tone of utter derision from their voice, "then why would I not also use magic to appear simultaneously at every commercial outlet on Earth?" A pause. "Well?"

++the g'norr are your friends—welcome them++

The youngling's eyes glazed, regarding Sneet blankly for a moment. Then:

"Shove it up your arse!" he squealed, and was off and running for the exit before Sneet's download could finish providing a translation.

FLASH!

"ARGH!"

— arcs of incandescent superheated plasma melting through the sides of descending troop carriers —

"Sorry!"

"Kid's already gone, Trevor," Tina called out.

"Really?" Trevor straightened up and blinked. "I could have sworn… Huh. Well, maybe Santa needs to lose a bit of the old midsection, eh?" He chuckled, slapping a hand against his own arguably excessive belly. "I could have sworn all that extra padding was a kid!"

"Moron," Tina muttered to Sneet. "And how about the mouth on that kid! If *I'd* talked to adults that way when I was that age…"

"Immediate ritual disembowelment!" Sneet finished, nodding in agreement.

"What??"

"I…said nothing."

`subject escaped processing—unacceptable!`

<Apologies, but—>

`unacceptable!`

Sneet scowled at the cacophonous mass of primates nearby.

<I wish to raise a concern with Central>

`proceed`

<Even with the reduced capacity of these REUs, the algorithm should be fully accessing the human cortex, with my

reinforcement simply giving an extra 'push'. However, that last youngling seemed to ignore the algorithm altogether>

A pause.

`observation supported`

<Well, I understand this supposition contradicts accepted wisdom regarding Level Three civilisations, but…could sensory overstimulation due to the crowded location be interfering with processing? I mean, is it possible that a Level Three species could be so easily distracted?>

A longer pause.

`observation…provisionally supported—a note has been uploaded to central`

Frek! Sneet thought. *How did these humans achieve a Level Three civilisation with such impaired cognitive wiring? This is what comes from Central rushing into this mission without full intel…*

"For what it's worth," Tina said, noting Sneet's dark expression, "I thought you handled that pretty well."

Sneet nodded curtly. "I…appreciate your evaluation. Thank you," they added, after a quick sift.

Tina smiled, before moving to acquire the next youngling. "This is Nigel, Santa."

"Greetings, Nigel. And what do you wish me to bring you for Christmas?"

++the g'norr are your friends—welcome them— love, serve, obey++

Without making optical contact with Sneet, the youngling pulled a folded-up piece of paper from the breast pocket of his immaculately pressed button-up shirt. "I," he said, with an air of self-importance that Sneet thought surpassed that of most System Overlords, "have a list."

Sneet smiled tightly. "Indeed?"

"I want," Nigel continued, unfolding the paper into something resembling a full-sized stellar map, "a PlayStation Five, a red Prevelo bicycle, a Spider-Man Aqua-Attack figure, a premium badminton set, a boxed set of Derwent artists' coloured pencils, a Racin' Rager Speedboat, a pair of Nike Air Max Plus Light Photography Printed Mesh sneakers, a trampoline, a Totem-Tennis set, a SpyraThree Water Blaster, an iPhone Sixteen, the new Fortnite game for PlayStation Five, a Fortnite logo 3D bedside lamp, a Fortnite pencil case—"

"Enough!" Sneet snapped. The youngling looked up, a look of annoyance wrinkling his chubby features. To Sneet's dismay, Nigel's eyes seemed bright and unbothered by the algorithm.

<The Id is strong with this one. Flag with Central as an addendum to previous note>

```
    flagged
++the g'norr are your friends—welcome them—
love, serve, obey++
```

<Let me tell you what I shall bring,> Sneet projected, leaning in towards the youngling. *<I shall bring the g'norr, your new masters. Do you understand?>*

The youngling glanced down at his list, then back at Sneet.

<Well? Who do you serve?>

Nigel shrugged

<It is the g'norr, yes?> Sneet urged.

Nigel frowned. "I suppose."

Sneet nodded triumphantly.

"Smile for the camera!" Trevor miraculously remembered to call out. Sneet averted their optics. There was a slight pause. "There's still a kid there, right?"

"Yes!" Tina confirmed tersely.

FLASH!

<Now forget, until otherwise directed> Sneet ordered. "You may go!" they added out loud, pointing towards the exit.

Nigel dismounted and trudged away, glancing back at Sneet with an unreadable expression on his face.

do not deviate from mission specifications—
acquiescing to youngling demands supports the
algorithm

<*But—*>

do not deviate

Sneet huffed in annoyance, turning to regard their next subject.

"This is Vanessa, Santa."

"Greetings, Vanessa. What do you wish me to bring you for Christmas?"

++the g'norr are your friends—welcome them—
love, serve, obey++

The youngling mumbled something.

"I cannot hear you," Sneet said impatiently. "You are speaking too quietly to be heard by the human ear, which is of course what I am equipped with. Please speak more loudly and clearly."

"Wan' Daddy."

<*What?*>

await clarification

"I see," Sneet said cautiously. "Kindly provide further explanation."

Vanessa's lip quivered. "Mummy says Daddy's in Heaven, an' I really miss him, an' Mummy still cries at night 'cos she misses him too, an' if you bring Daddy back for Christmas I don' mind if you give my presents to some'n' else." To Sneet's alarm, tears began to well up in the corner of the youngling's eyes. *"Please?"*

<Context?>

`hypothesis: the male parent of the youngling is deceased—she is requesting the parent be revived`

<Oh, for—even this stupid primate must realise that—>
`acquiesce`

Freksake! "Vanessa," Sneet began sternly.

The youngling stared miserably, looking not unlike a skutchling newly separated from its brood queen, and Sneet felt a sudden twinge. They hesitated, then took a deep breath. "Vanessa. I regret to advise that I will be unable to—"

`do not deviate!—acquiesce!`

"That is, I do not believe it is physically possible for me to—"

The youngling began to sob, tears pouring down her reddening cheeks.

— the weeping of shattered soldiers, bleeding out into the dirt —

`expressing grief`

<Yes! I worked that out for myself!>

Hence my being assigned to this ridiculous mission, Sneet thought to themself sourly. "Hush!" they hissed.

Vanessa ceased crying, her breath hitching brokenly.

Sneet performed a hasty sift. *<I cannot access any relevant advisory information! Please assist!>*

`searching...`

A pause.

<Well??>

`central    trusts    in    your    experience    and abilities`

Sneet opened their mouth, then closed it again, then thought some very bad words, then took a moment to collect their thoughts. "Vanessa. Listen to me."

`++the g'norr are your friends—welcome them++`

The youngling's eyes misted over slightly.

"Death comes to all biological life," Sneet went on, in what they hoped was a kind but matter-of-fact tone, "and no known power in the universe can permanently reverse the process, even with expert medical application of invasive organobionics, or parasites that can override neurological function. Therefore it is best for you to simply spend a moment of silence in memory of the fallen, then forget them as best you can and rejoin the battle—er, that is, continue on with your life. Without dying. Until you inevitably *do* die, of course." They paused. "I hope this advice assists you in dealing with your loss."

Behind them, Sneet heard Tina hiss "What the actual *fuck*, dude??"

The youngling continued to stare up at Sneet for moment. Then she began to wail loudly.

FLASH!

"ARGH!"

"Sorry! I thought she was smiling for the camera!"

Sneet squinted angrily through the dark spots strobing their vision. Several of the waiting adult humans were regarding them suspiciously. One particular female, undoubtedly Vanessa's mother, glared at them from the sidelines. "Oh, very well!" Sneet growled irritably. "I shall bring you your daddy for Christmas!"

The crying ceased instantly. Vanessa beamed at Sneet.

<And your new masters, the g'norr!> Sneet projected, without enthusiasm. *<To love, serve and obey…etcetera!>*

She nodded excitedly.

<Now forget, until otherwise directed> "Go now." Sneet's leg was quickly vacated, then re-occupied. "Greetings—" they began, then let out a bellow of disgust as hot, evil-smelling liquid began to soak through the left leg of their trousers. *"Trask devour you, filthy demonspawn!"* The youngling fled, squealing.

FLASH!

"WHY??" Sneet roared, visions of imploding battledroids flickering before their traumatised optics.

"Sorry! I thought he was still on your knee!"

Tina tapped Sneet on the shoulder. "You should probably go and clean up."

"Really? Had you not suggested it, I may well have sat here in blissful ignorance for the remainder of the day, marinating in urine!"

"Ah, shove it up your arse, John. I'm just trying to help. You know where the bathroom is." She jerked a thumb towards the door from which Sneet had entered the quadrangle. "Go clean up, and I'll stall the mob."

Inwardly cursing, Sneet rose and stalked towards the door, the sensation of sodden fabric slapping against their leg reminding them of the horrors of jungle-borne wet-rot. Behind them, they could hear Tina doing her best to cover their departure. "Santa just has to go and check on his reindeer—" wails of protest from younglings and adults alike, "—but he'll be back very soon, so if I could just ask you to be a little bit patient…"

At this moment I would ecstatically trade having to deal with these human younglings for the horrors of unarmed combat against a nest of raging swarfs. Swarfs do not demand gifts. Swarfs do not tell you to shove anything up your arse. They certainly do not urinate upon you, unless involuntarily during torture. They just die when you shoot them. Frek, even skutchlings *have more self-control than these youngling primates!*

My poor, sweet skutchlings—

Utterly preoccupied, Sneet almost collided with Jeremy, who was looking extremely harried. Sneet briefly wondered if that was Jeremy's default expression. "I was just coming to get you." Jeremy glanced down. "Oh dear. Did a child pee on you?"

"Your powers of observation astound me."

"Right. Well, occupational hazard, I suppose. Anyway," Jeremy continued, ignoring Sneet's glare, "I've had a complaint from one of the parents, and I just need you to come and help smooth the water a bit. It shouldn't take a moment. Then you can go and clean up." He offered what Sneet's download suggested was a wholly insincere smile.

Sneet narrowed their optics suspiciously. "Would it not be more sanitary, and less unpleasant for all, for me to wash the urine out of my clothes *before* meeting with the complainant?"

Jeremy licked his lips. "The complainant is being rather…insistent."

Sneet glanced longingly towards the door leading to the bathroom. "Very well. But let us make this quick. My skin is beginning to burn." How the acidic liquid had managed to seep all the way through a thick layer of fabric *and* several layers of human-looking syntheskin was utterly beyond Sneet, but it was an issue they very much intended to raise with Central.

Jeremy nodded and motioned Sneet to follow him, heading off towards a small alcove further away from the door to the bathroom than Sneet would have liked. As they got closer, and Sneet saw who was occupying the alcove, their pulmonary glands sank. It was the youngling named Nigel, accompanied by two human adults, presumably his parents.

"What sorta crap you been tellin' my kid?" demanded Nigel's father, a large, hirsute specimen with a conversely hairless cranium, wearing a paint-spattered flannelette shirt.

"Sir, please!" Jeremy raised a placating hand. "I'm sure this is just a simple misunderstanding. Let's give Santa a chance to explain, shall we?"

Nigel's father's face turned a shade of purple that Sneet's download identified as atypical in humans. "You callin' my son a *liar?!*" Several bystanders turned to stare. "You callin' him a goddamn *liar?!*"

"Nicholas darling, please don't make a scene," chided Nigel's mother, an elegant woman as immaculately dressed as her son.

Nigel's father ignored her, pushing a bloated finger so deeply into the front of Sneet's suit that it pressed painfully against their thoracic plate. Sneet fought the urge to remove the offending finger from the offender's hand. "My kid says Santa refused to bring him any toys!"

"I'm sure that's not…" Jeremy turned to Sneet, eyebrows raised. "Santa?"

"I did not refuse," Sneet said, truthfully.

"I started reading my list," Nigel whined, "and he wouldn't listen!"

Nigel's father glowered at Sneet. "Well?"

Jeremy favoured Nigel with a patronising smile, "Look, I'm sure we all understand that Santa doesn't like to actually *promise* to bring what you ask for, because sometimes he runs out of particular toys, so promising could put *Santa—*" and here he glanced pointedly at Nigel's father, "—in an awkward position. But that's not the same thing as *refusing* to bring toys, is it?"

Nigel's mother looked up at her husband, rubbing his arm gently. "There you are, darling. It was all just a silly miscommunication, that's all."

Nigel's father seemed to relax slightly, his facial hue shifting from almost black to merely aubergine.

Jeremy turned back to Nigel. "So that's why Santa just says he'll *try* to bring what you asked for."

Ah, frek, Sneet thought.

Nigel's lip started to quiver. "He didn't say anything like that! All he said was that he was going to bring some new masters who I had to serve, and they were called the gnaw!"

Sneet stared at the youngling. *Impossible!*

"Gnaw?" Nigel's father growled at Sneet. "Masters? What kinda crap is this? You some kinda pervert?"

<Priority! Check REU for errors!>

```
checking—no errors—reinforce processing
```

Sneet quickly crouched down beside Nigel. *<Forget all that was told to you of the g'norr! Forget!>*

"I'm sure Santa wouldn't have said anything of the sort!" Jeremy protested.

"Goddamn it!" Nigel's father snarled. "Call my kid a liar again and I'll shove my fist so far up your arse—!"

What is this obsession humans have with arses?

<Do you understand, youngling? Forget until otherwise directed!>

"Nicholas, please, do remember your blood pressure!"

"You awful man!" Everyone turned to regard the distressed-looking human female striding towards them, dragging the youngling Vanessa alongside her. "How *could* you!"

"Please, madam!" Jeremy now seemed on the verge of panic. People were actually leaving the queue to Santa's grotto to hurry over and investigate the escalating situation in the alcove. Sneet was reminded far too vividly of the experience of being pinned down in a trench by approaching enemy footsoldiers. Even the security guard began to drift across, hand hovering idly over his holster.

The newly arrived female glared at Jeremy whilst levelling an accusing finger at Sneet. "How *dare* your Santa tell Vanessa her father's coming home for Christmas? Her father's *dead!*"

There was a shocked intake of breath from the gathering crowd.

Then silence.

Then a single voice from the back of the crowd said: "Ohhh, shit!"

`prioritise reinforcement`

<*I know!*> "Do you understand?" Sneet hissed to Nigel. <*Forget!*>.

"Forget what?" Nigel whined plaintively. "The gnaw, or the presents?"

<*The g'norr! Forget the g'norr!*>

"Excuse me?" Another human couple appeared beside Nigel's parents. "Sorry, we couldn't help overhearing. Troy—" the female of the couple nodded towards her own youngling, "—said exactly the same thing about Santa bringing the gnaw, or gnawing on him, or something. That was right, wasn't it, Troy?"

Troy nodded. "The gnaw. To love, serve and obey."

"We thought he was just mucking around. Y'know, like kids do. But then we heard what *you* were saying, and—"

`reinforce processing`

<*I KNOW!*> Sneet spun on their haunches, glaring at Troy. <*Forget! I command you to forget!*>

"*Excuse* me?" Troy's father snapped. "*What* did you just say to my son??"

Oh, so now *the processing works!* Sneet stood up and met the human's gaze unblinkingly. "I…said nothing."

"I certainly didn't hear him say anything, darling," Troy's mother interjected.

"That's because my hearing's better than yours now, Carol." Troy's father held a finger to one of his ears, indicating a small electronic device nestled there. "These new hearing aids pick up *everything!*"

"I…didn't even see his lips move, Simon…"

Troy's father frowned. "Well…you know these Santas often have other acting jobs. This one can probably do ventriloquism…"

<Ventriloquism?>

The download offered an explanation.

<I…am I even awake *right now??>*

"She's been in therapy for *months!*" Vanessa's mother wailed. "She misses her father *so much!* Do you have any idea how much damage you've done? *Do you?!*"

"Look, please, madam," Jeremy said desperately, "I'm sure this is all just a huge misunderstanding!"

`maintain control of situation`

<How? Advise!>

`assessing...assessing...please wait...`

"I'm so very sorry for your loss." Nigel's mother laid a comforting hand on Vanessa's mother's arm. "It must be so difficult for you both. And at Christmas, too."

"Well, thank you." Vanessa's mother managed a tight smile, then shot a glance at her daughter to check if she was listening before leaning closer to Nigel's mother and whispering, at a volume Sneet felt could have raised the fallen, "Look, he's not actually dead—that's just what I told *her*. To protect her, y'know? Bastard ran away with the TV repairman. I *wish* he was dead!"

`assessing...please wait...`

Sneet furiously straightened their back, allowing their interlocked sternal rings to separate and expand. The surrounding crowd backed away slightly at the sight of Santa suddenly appearing to grow a full half-metre taller, visibly straining the stitching of his crimson suit. "ALL OF YOU!" Sneet shouted angrily, sweeping the crowd with a glare. "Give me your attention!" *<Priority! Maximise output and range of REU!>*

`++THE G'NORR ARE YOUR FRIENDS—WELCOME THEM—LOVE, SERVE, OBEY++`

The eyes of the crowd, younglings and adults alike, became vacant and unfocussed. There was a moment of silence.

Then…

One of the younglings standing nearby—*Charles*, Sneet recalled bitterly—blinked slowly, smirked, pointed at Vanessa and snorted with spiteful glee. "Your mummy says your daddy ran *awaa-aay!*" he sang.

Vanessa immediately burst into tears.

"Oh, you little shit!" Vanessa's mother spat.

'Hoy!" snapped another woman, presumably Charles' mother. "Don't you dare speak to my son like that!"

"*Be silent!*" Sneet snarled. "All of you! Look at me and hear my words!"

++THE G'NORR ARE YOUR FRIENDS—WELCOME THEM— LOVE, SERVE, OBEY++

<OBEY AND FORGET!>

"Your daddy ran *awaa-aay!* Your daddy ran *awaa-aay!*" Charles repeated mockingly. "*My* mummy an' daddy an' me all live in our house *together*, an' th' smorning I went in their room an' Daddy was jumping up an' down on Mummy's tummy while he was lying on top of her an' Mummy was crying really loud an' I smacked Daddy on the bum an' yelled BAD

DADDY!—*WAAAAAAAAH!"* he added, as his crimson-faced mother yoinked him by the neck of his shirt and dashed away.

`reinforce processing—still assessing situational requirements...`

"Vanessa, sweetie, darling!" Vanessa's mother crouched down protectively by her child. "Are you okay, sweetie?"

Vanessa choked on her sobs, took a deep breath and let out a nerve-shredding scream—

—a terrifying screech shreds the silence of the savannah. Fighting the urge to flee, Sneet assumes the warrior's pose, a range of bladed weapons gripped in their tentacles, one claw holding a ten-shot pulse bazooka, the other lightly pressed to the tab of the suicide grenade slung from their harness as the swarm of klettan arachnoids gallops towards them –

"This is all your fault!" Vanessa's mother barked at Jeremy, whose face had now assumed the colour and consistency of gelatine. "I'm going to *sue* this mall, and you and your Santa personally, for *every cent you own!* Do you have any idea how much therapy *costs? Do you??"*

"Madam, *please!"* Jeremy begged weakly.

"What sorta setup you runnin' here, you sonofabitch!" Nigel's father demanded, thrusting his chest into Jeremy's personal space.

"Sir, please, if you'd just give me a moment to—"

"Sir?" The security guard moved closer, eyeing Nigel's father warily as he unclipped his holster. "Could you please take a couple of steps back?"

"You called security on me??" Nigel's father squealed.

"What?? No!! I've been here with you for the last five minutes!! When could I possibly have—??" Jeremy directed a pacifying gesture towards the guard. "It's okay, Roger, I've got this under control."

`reinforce processing`

Sneet gritted their teeth. *This cannot be happening! How can these accursed primates possibly resist reprogramming when the algorithm is so clearly being received and understood? Unless...*

No. Impossible.

Sneet bent down over Nigel. "Tell me," they hissed urgently, "what do you wish me to bring you for Christmas?"

Nigel took an involuntary step backwards, then puffed out his chest defiantly. "I *told* you! I want a PlayStation Five, a red Prevelo bicycle, a Spider-Man Aqua-Attack figure—"

<*NO! Listen and obey!*> Sneet stared deeply into Nigel's eyes. *<I shall bring new masters, the g'norr! That is what you want for Christmas!>*

++THE G'NORR ARE YOUR FRIENDS—WELCOME THEM—LOVE, SERVE, OBEY++

Nigel's expression went blank for a moment. Then he shook his head. "I want a *PlayStation Five!*"

An icy claw seemed to close around Sneet's pulmonary glands. They slowly stood up again and swept the crowd with a look of utter dismay. *<Frek! The one time Central fails to perform due diligence in gathering intel on a newly discovered civilisation...! These humans do not operate like other previously-encountered sentient species, ruled by Id with a trace of Ego! Against all logic, they exist simultaneously in both states—sentient and animal! Sufficiently intelligent for the algorithm to tap into their central cortex, yet synchronously influenced by such levels of personal craving that—when reprogramming commences—their animalistic fixations immediately engage and negate the effects of re-education! Which means—>*

Sneet quivered.

<—which means there is no way this mission can succeed!>

supposition supported—a note has been uploaded to central—await feedback—proceed with reinforcement

<IT IS NOT WORKING!>

`additional verbal endorsement suggested`

With a growing sense of dread, Sneet bent down to face Nigel again. "Nigel! *Listen and focus!*" *<You! Will! Accept! The g'norr!>*

"*Daddeee!!* He's talking about the gnaw again!"

"*Sonofabitch!*" Nigel's father delivered a sharp shove to Jeremy's shoulder. "You better get your Santa in line right now, or I'm gonna—!"

"Sir!" The security guard now had his weapon drawn, a snub-nosed plastic firearm pointed unsteadily at the floor. "Move back *right now!* I won't tell you again!"

"*I want a PlayStation Five! Give me a PlayStation Five, you stupid man!*"

Sneet reared up, glaring at the youngling. *I could crush you like a mollusc! Disembowel you with my spurs! Tear you apart! Atomise you!*

`alert!—intentions exceed allowable beha-viour!—stand down!—stand down!`

<But—!>

`a report has been uploaded to central!—disciplinary action will be advised!`

And just like that, Sneet's fury evaporated.

<I...comply>

Coward! whispered a tiny voice in their hindbrain.

I know, Sneet thought miserably. *I am a coward. I do not stand up for myself. That is why I acquiesced to this ridiculous mission. That is why I cannot even assert my dominance over a human youngling. Because nobody respects me.*

Not even myself.

"PlayStation!!"

"Sonofabitch!"

"Sir!!"

"You awful man!!"

Something deep in Sneet's cerebral lobe snapped.

"One more word, demonspawn," they snarled, glaring at Nigel, *"and I shall tear you open and spatter your guts across that artificial vegetation!"* Without breaking optical contact, Sneet pointed a claw towards the plastic tree beside Santa's throne.

There was a shocked silence. Then:

"DADDEEEEE!!"

"SONOFABITCH!!" Nigel's father screamed, charging towards Sneet. *"I'M GONNA KILL YOU!!"*

Sneet spun around to face the oncoming human. "I accept your challenge! In fact, I offer you the first strike, you foul, hairy, under-evolved *primate*!"

"I mean, the number of times *I've* wanted to tell a customer what I really thought of them…" Tina said, holding the icepack firmly to Sneet's optical socket. "But to actually *do* it? Shit, man, I don't know whether that makes you a hero or a complete nutter, but mad props either way."

Sneet gave a non-committal grunt.

"And it was pretty cool seeing Nigel's dad get shot," Tina continued. "I'm assuming you missed that, given you were slightly comatose at the time."

"Was his death drawn out and agonising?" Sneet asked hopefully.

"Um…no. Roger tazed him, he did a little dance, then shat himself and fell over." Tina pulled the icepack away and frowned. "Huh. You're not even bruised. Given how hard he belted you, I thought—"

"I shall be fine, thank you," Sneet snapped, twisting on the toilet seat so they could turn their face away. The syntheskin had certain limits of realism. Underneath, their own flesh was no doubt turning an interesting shade of orange.

"Well, okay, if you're sure." Tina glanced at Jeremy, who was slumped against the cubicle door. From outside the bathroom, echoing up the corridor, came a steady collective roar of discontent. "Guess I'd better get out there and try to calm the animals. Again. I really don't get paid enough for this, Jeremy. And we clearly need a first aid station closer to Santa's grotto."

"Yes! Thank you!" Jeremy stood back to let Tina past as she left the cubicle. "I'll bring it up with senior management!"

"Bullshit, Jeremy. Bullshit."

"What on *earth* were you *thinking?*" Jeremy demanded as Tina left. "You…you just can't *talk* to customers like that! I *know* the children are a mob of self-entitled little so-and-sos! I *know* the parents are even worse! But good golly! Threatening a *kid?* In front of his *parents?* And then challenging the parent to a *fight?*" He shook his head in utter disbelief. "What on *earth* is *wrong* with you?"

Sneet huffed wearily.

Jeremy rubbed his eyes, then gave an exasperated shrug. "Well. I've done some damage control. Gave the parents some vouchers. But…I mean, if it hadn't been for the fact that you were the one who was assaulted, the police probably would have arrested you for causing an affray! Frankly, I should absolutely fire you, except—" he stopped abruptly.

"Except that you have no other Santas to call upon," Sneet said quietly.

Jeremy made a nervously dismissive gesture. "That's neither here nor there. We're wasting time, so let's get you back out there, pronto!"

Sneet looked up sharply. "I beg your pardon?"

Jeremy gestured towards the bathroom door. "Get back out there! That crowd's going to tear the mall apart if Santa doesn't hop to it!"

Sneet opened their mouth to protest.

priority!—incoming from central: abort mission!—all operatives recalled!—abort mission!

<A complete *recall? Immediate? Confirm!>*

confirmed—action as soon as possible without alerting humans

Something major must have occurred, Sneet realised; something far exceeding their own abject failure. They stood up gingerly and favoured Jeremy with a smile that was just slightly too wide to be comfortably accommodated by their human disguise. Jeremy blanched and took a step back. "Jeremy," Sneet said, "I regret to inform you that I shall not 'hop to it'. Nor shall I any longer subject myself to the frankly—" they sifted for the appropriate local term, "—*inhumane* conditions of this workplace. I hereby resign my position as the Santa of Frankston Mall, and will be leaving the premises as soon as I have attended to my urine-soaked trousers."

Jeremy turned paler still. "No, hang on, wait a moment, just…look, we can discuss this after—"

"We cannot." Sneet pointed to the door. "Kindly leave."

Jeremy gawped for a moment, then pulled an expression that (according to Sneet's download) might have indicated either determination or constipation, and folded his arms across his chest. "Unacceptable. You are not leaving this mall until the end of your contracted shift at seven pm tonight. And I am not leaving your side until that time comes. Understand?"

Sneet briefly considered using the atomiser. But no; their own disappearance would cause enough suspicion without the additional mystery of a missing mid-level department store employee.

`priority: abort mission as soon as possible without alerting humans`

Which meant—

Sneet quivered. "But…there are at least a hundred of them out there!"

"A hundred? Goodness, yes. There *are* at least a hundred. *Now…*"

Iceworms crawled down Sneet's notochord. "What do you mean, *'now'*?"

"Oh, gosh, you really *must* be new at this. Those kids out there are just the early birds, the ones whose parents camp on the doorstep until the mall opens. By the time we close tonight we'll have had at least a *thousand* kids come through!"

"A thousand??"

"Indeed. So you'd best pull yourself together. Santa's Grotto has only been open for—" Jeremy consulted the timekeeping device on his wrist, "—forty-five minutes. Which means you still have seven hours and forty-five minutes to go. Not including your thirty-minute lunch break."

"Seven—?" Sneet teetered, steadying themself against the cubicle doorframe. "But—I do not *want* to!" they whined.

Jeremy's eye twitched slightly, and the corners of his mouth tweaked upwards into a smile that even Sneet could tell wasn't really a smile. "You know, I've just realised that I never actually asked you your name."

"John."

"Ah. Right. Well, John," the not-smile widened slightly, "I'll tell you what—you can take not wanting to do it, bundle it up nicely…and shove it up your arse." The eye twitched again. "How does that sound?"

Sneet stared at Jeremy.

Jeremy stared back.

"One moment, please," Sneet croaked, then staggered to the far cubicle, demagnetised the lock, and leaned across the cocoon to grab the half-empty bottle of scotch. *<Short-term effects upon g'norr physiology?>*

`anticipating light physical anaesthesia, major decline in mental acuity–`

<Excellent!> Sneet took a swig, choked, gasped, swigged again.

Jeremy appeared in the cubicle doorway. "My God! Are you *drinking?*"

Sneet carefully considered their answer. "Yes."

Jeremy clapped his hands to his head. "Oh my—! They don't *pay* me enough to put up with this! You can't go out there *drunk!*"

"So get someone else," Sneet growled, as an unfamiliar yet pleasant warmth bled from their gullet into their extremities. They took a final huge swig, then placed the now empty bottle atop the cistern with exaggerated precision, before sitting down on the toilet and attempting to wring as much urine from their trouser leg as possible. A thick yellow pool began to collect on the tiled floor at their feet.

"There *is* no-one else!" Jeremy spluttered.

Sneet glanced at him blearily. "Quite."

Jeremy glared at them. "You're just as bad as Stan!"

Sneet stood up and pushed past Jeremy, moving unsteadily towards the sink to wash the urine off their claws. "Stan," they slurred, "is obviously far more intelligent than either of us gave him credit for."

Sneet had never seen a superior officer so angry as Kevlaar looked right now.

The Fleetlord crouched silently in their web, glaring at their display. Sneet, who hadn't even been acknowledged yet, stood at the opposite end of the table, shifting uncomfortably.

After a very long silence, they coughed hesitantly.

Kevlaar looked up sharply and fixed Sneet with a look of absolute rage. *"A COMPLETE FAILURE!!"* they screamed.

"Every! Single! Operative! All encountering exactly the same range of issues as yourself! Failures, every last one of them!"

And how is that my *fault, you bloated malcontent?* The thought, angry and unthinkably insubordinate, flashed through Sneet's hindbrain before they could clamp down upon it. A small bleat of shock escaped their throat.

Kevlaar narrowed their optics. "You have something to say?"

Sneet bowed their cranium. *Will I ever see my farm again?* "No, Fleetlord. Apologies."

Coward!

Kevlaar regarded Sneet suspiciously for a moment, then turned their attention back to their display. "You may count yourself fortunate that Central lays all fault with their own intelligence and tech. However, despite this abysmal failure, they still assert the basic existing plan can be successful…once some adjustments have been made. Based upon the intel gleaned from Operation Santa, they have already begun to modify the algorithm and adjust the mission specs to target other widely held local ideologies. Going forward, operatives will deal with human younglings on a *completely* one-on-one basis, to eliminate all possible sources of distraction for those subjects."

They pointed towards Sneet's display. "Observe the amended specifications."

Sneet stepped forward and regarded the scrolling text. "Operation Easter Bunny," they said tonelessly. "Operation Tooth Fairy."

"You will accept the mission?" It was barely a question; more a traditional invitation to comply.

Sneet stared blankly at Kevlaar. *So very like a human youngling. Petulant. Demanding. Disrespectful. When was the last time* you *saw combat, Fleetlord? Was it decades ago? Centuries? Have you, in fact,* ever *personally faced an enemy on the battlefield?* The screams of dying warriors echoed in their hindbrain. A tight smile tweaked the corners of their mouth, then slowly stretched into a full, toothy grin.

Kevlaar shrank back into their web at the sight.

Still grinning, Sneet slowly leaned forward and pressed their upper claws flat against the tabletop as they glared directly into Kevlaar's optics.

"With *all due respect*, Fleetlord," Sneet said, meaning every word of it, "you can take this mission…and shove it up your arse!"

DEDICATION

To Mum and Dad, who supported me in everything I ever did, and whom I miss every single day.

To the friends, colleagues, readers, editors, booksellers and fellow authors who have supported and encouraged me throughout twenty-five years of being a published author. Thanks especially to Bill Congreve, Cat Sparks, Robert Hood, Sarah Endacott, KM Stevenson, Lindy Cameron, Katya de Beccara and Narrelle M. Harris.

To Ian 'Blackie' Cummins, Lee Battersby, Matt Cheetham, and others of their ilk, who help keep my mind sharp by subjecting me to their absolute nonsense. Keep it up: it's far more entertaining than Sudoku.

To Luke Aldred, for taking a vague and boring cover concept of mine, and turning it into the absolute masterpiece adorning the front of this book.

To my cats, MacReady and Ripley, who continue to be the worst flatmates a guy ever had. Get a job, you bums.

To my kids, neither of whom yet show any inclination to put me into a substandard nursing home when I inevitably lose my marbles. I love you both beyond my ability to express.

To my partner's family, all of whom continue to overwhelm me with their generosity and support. You are all refreshing pools of crystal water in what at times feels like an endless sandy desert filled with lizard shit.

And finally, to Sarah, who holds my heart every single day. You complete me.

ABOUT THE AUTHOR

Chuck McKenzie was born in 1970 and is still not dead. He is an award-nominated author of numerous science fiction and horror stories, and he hopes one day to be described by his neighbours as having seemed like such a nice man. You can stalk him on Instagram at **@chuck.mckenzie.author**

ALSO BY CHUCK MCKENZIE

Worlds Apart (Novel, Hybrid Publishers 1999).

AustrAlien Absurdities: Comic Tales of Science-Fiction, Fantasy & Horror by Australian Authors (Anthology, co-edited with Tansy Rayner-Roberts, Agog! Press 2001).

Confessions of a Pod Person (Collection, MirrorDanse Editions 2005).

Conversations With My Cat (Collection, co-authored with MacReady McKenzie and Ripley McKenzie, Daft Notions 2023).

The Dark Man, By Referral and Less Pleasant Tales (Collection, Daft Notions 2024)

Praise for *The Dark Man, By Referral and Less Pleasant Tales*

Creepy excellence with all the scary stuff included.
Goodreads

These fantastical, psychological horror tales will suck you in with McKenzie's warm style of writing, engage you in their oh so familiar scenarios and shock you with their twisty, turny endings. You will be just another fish dangling in a hook once you start this collection. A great collection of stories that will leave in tears, whether that be laughter, shock, or surprise.
Stephen Ormsby, author of Long Lost Song

I love single author short story collections
and books like this are the reason why.
Goodreads

Dark, disturbing and enthralling. These tales are both personal and relatable. The characters feel real, just like you and me, despite the bizarre situations they find themselves in. Spooky, entertaining and weird.
Steven Paulsen, author of Shadows on the Wall

Chuck McKenzie's collection of short stories and flash fiction... runs the gamut of sci-fi and horror, hitting both comedic and horrifying notes equally well. Keep up the good work, Chuck, you've made another fan right here!
Goodreads

Chuck McKenzie has long been one of my favourite short story writers. McKenzie offers a unique voice with his fiction, and this collection delivers his trademark mix of horror and dark fiction infused with a deft sense of tongue-in-cheek humour.
Mark Smith-Briggs, author and reviewer

Very scary and entertaining, thought provoking and creepy.
Highly recommended.
Goodreads

What the Cool Cats said about
Conversations With My Cat

A must for people who like cats, people who despise cats, cats who like people, cats who despise people… basically everybody. Except children: as the book jacket warns, these cats are potty mouths.
Five stars.
Pete Aldin, author of the Envoys Universe series

This made me laugh so loud and often, the cats left the room.
Goodreads

As a fellow cat owner (or cat servant) I needed to read this. I am so glad I did. This book is so relatable and laugh out loud funny.
@ashisalwaysreading, bookblogger

Every cat owner (I mean cat servant) needs to read this one. MacReady—with his witty, aloof, snarky and altogether hysterical 'typical cat' responses to his housemate Chuck—is great.
Goodreads

Conversations With My Cat is full of dialogue very familiar to every cat owner in the world. It's no coincidence that it's also full of the deep fondness that humans have for their contrary
and sometimes bossy best friends.
Narrelle M. Harris, author of *The Opposite of Life*

A good reminder to us of the feline persuasion of the many trials and tribulations we face in dealing with our humans.
Five purrs and two paws up.
Princess Fuzzypants, Feline Social Media Starlet

As much as I hate cats, and despise narratives in which domestic pets speak both coherently and articulately, I found this book to be a delightful romp!
Maxwell Q. Littledog, Canine Facebook Influencer

Conversations With My Cat had me grinning from the acknowledgements page onwards. If you are a cat person, this will prove everything you ever imagined about cats. If you are a dog person, it will prove everything you ever imagined about cats.
Claire Low, artist

Publisher of the Niche, the Oddball, the Unsettling…

Small press publisher operating out of Melbourne, Australia.

Current and forthcoming publications include science fiction and horror titles, management guides, single-author collections, novels and novellas, and funny cat books.

For more information and to purchase our titles go to:
www.daftnotions.com

www.ingramcontent.com/pod-product-compliance
Lightning Source LLC
Chambersburg PA
CBHW020534120726
47904CB00003B/1079